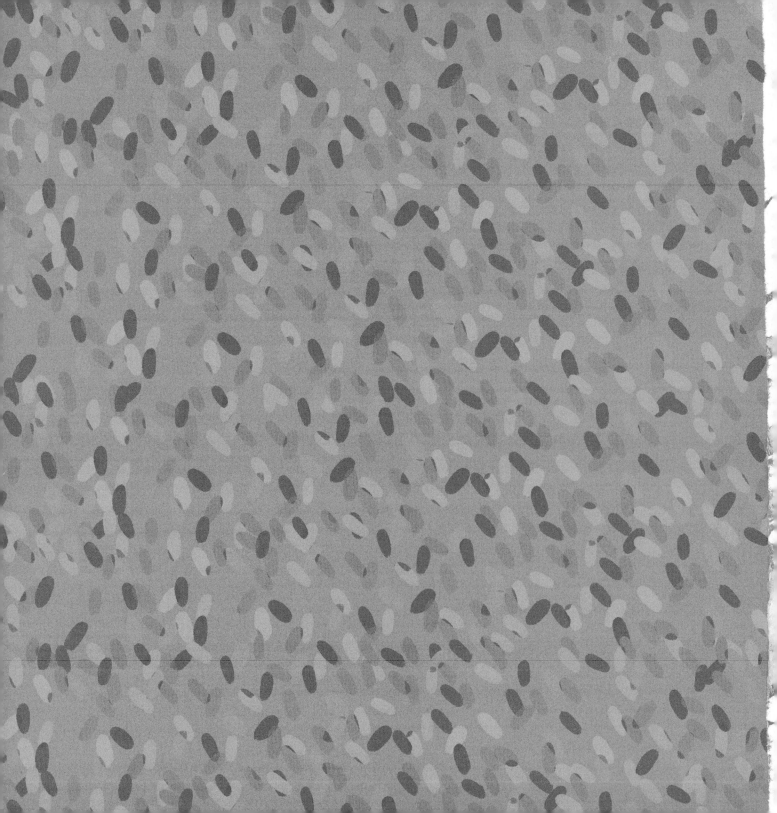

The Way we say Hello

By ANDREA DENISH Illustrated by BLUEBEAN

STARRY FOREST

A special day. A special place.
How will you greet a special face?

A wink?

A pat?

A tap-tap tug?

A wave?

A shake?

A big bear hug?

How will **YOU** say **HELLO**?

Like an English gent who stops to chat, say, "Good day," and tip your hat.

Or wear a crown and wiggle your wrist,
give your wave a royal twist.

Meet cheek to cheek and say, "Bonjour."
Kiss once, kiss twice, three times or more!

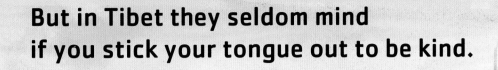

But in Tibet they seldom mind
if you stick your tongue out to be kind.

How will **YOU** say **HELLO**?

In Japan, to bow politely, face your friend and bend down slightly.

Or, like the Māori, greet your guest
nose to nose with foreheads pressed.

Say hello Big Island style,
spread Aloha with your smile.

Or let your inner light shine through,
bid, "Namaste — I honor you."

How will **YOU** say **HELLO**?

Tug your hat and stand up proudly,
give 'em all a Texas "HOWDY!"

Or take a trip to Guatapé,
where greetings match the time of day.

Hola

שלום
(Shalom)

Привет
(privet)

Ciao!

ΓΕΙΑ ΣΟU
(YASSOU)

AHOJ!

안녕
(Annyeong)

你好
(nǐ hǎo)

Guten Tag

Salut

你好
(Lí-hó)

How in the world will you say Hello?

Some hellos are seen, not heard.

Some don't need a single word.

Some hellos come by surprise.

Some shy,

some sweet, some . . .

. . . SUPERSIZED.

Make some noise when you arrive,
raise your hand and gimme five.

Over, under, snap, snap.
Wiggle, giggle, clap, clap.

How will **YOU** say **HELLO**?

You can shout hello across the yard,

or mail it in a greeting card.

Hellos can travel any place —
try launching one to outer space.

Now's your moment. Make a mark.

Spring to action. Light a spark.

Paint a picture. Hold a sign.
Add some shimmer, watch it shine.
Hang it up for all to know . . .

. . . this is how **WE** say **HELLO**.

MORE TO KNOW ABOUT SAYING HELLO!

HAT TIP

The hat tip gesture can be traced back to soldiers removing their helmets after leaving the battlefield. The gesture has come to represent a polite signal of respect and sincerity. It is most commonly associated with Western societies of the 19th and early 20th centuries.

WINDSOR WAVE

The British royal family greets crowds of onlookers with a wave. King Edward VIII complained that too much waving caused arm strain. A doctor's recommendation led to a simpler twisting motion known today as the "Windsor Wave."

KISSES ON THE CHEEK

Many places have a tradition of greeting friends, family, and even new acquaintances with kisses on each cheek. In some places, like Spain, two kisses (dos besos) are popular, but in other countries the greeting can include up to eight kisses!

HOWDY

"Howdy" is a short way of asking, "How do you do?"

STICKING OUT TONGUE

Tibet was once ruled by a king who was known for being unkind and was rumored to have a black tongue. In traditional Tibetan society, sticking your tongue out is proof that you are not like King Langdarma and has become a gesture of goodwill.

ALOHA

Aloha is more than a greeting — it's the spirit of treating others with love and kindness. "Aloha" is a way to welcome and wish others well.

NAMASTE

Press your palms together and give a slight bow. This peaceful Hindi greeting means "the divine within me honors the divine within you."

TIME OF DAY

Greetings that follow the time of day are used in many languages, like Spanish, the official language of Guatapé, Colombia. From sunrise to noon, say "buenos días / good morning." From noon to sunset, say "buenas tardes / good afternoon." And from sunset to sunrise, say "buenas noches / good night."

BOWING

Japan has a strong tradition of bowing to welcome, honor, or apologize. A small bow is used for close family and friends, while a deep bow is reserved for elders and high-ranking officials.

NOSE TO NOSE

The Māori of New Zealand welcome guests with the traditional hongi greeting. Two people press their noses together to symbolize sharing the breath of life.

SIGN LANGUAGE

Sign language is a way for people who are deaf or hard of hearing to communicate.

REUNIONS

Reunions bring families and friends together in one place. The largest family reunion on record happened in 2012, when 4,514 family members gathered in the French town of Saint-Paul-Mont-Penit, Vendée.

SPECIAL HANDSHAKES

Many people use personalized handshakes to greet one another. They may include snaps, claps, and pats on the back. Try making your own handshake with a friend.

BABIES

A newborn baby has a natural instinct to grasp someone's finger. It's their way of saying hello.

TECHNOLOGY

Technology allows people to send greetings anywhere — even into space! With a network of satellites called the TDRS, we send messages from Earth to astronauts at the International Space Station in an instant. (Or we can send a message from Earth to Mars — in 22 minutes or less!)

Book design by Chad W. Beckerman.

Title type design by Shauna Lynn Panczyszyn.

The illustrations were created with gouache, as well as digitally.

Starry Forest® is a registered trademark of Starry Forest Books, Inc.

This 2023 edition published by Starry Forest Books, Inc.

First edition 2023

Library of Congress Control Number 2022933083

ISBN 978-1-951784-24-9 (picture book)

ISBN 978-1-951784-95-9 (ebook)

Lot #: 2 4 6 8 10 9 7 5 3 1

Manufactured in China

09/22

STARRY
FOREST
BOOKS

Starry Forest Books, Inc.

P.O. Box 1797

217 East 70th Street

New York, NY 10021

starryforestbooks.com | @starryforestbks